To cats of all shapes and sizes!
—S.S.

To every dog that secretly wishes
they'd been born a cat
—B.S.

To cats of all shapes and sizes!
—S.S.

To every dog that secretly wishes
they'd been born a cat
—B.S.

I love cats!

Cats,

cats,

cats.

I
love
cats!

Wiggly cats,

giggly cats.

Wiry cats,

fiery cats.

Dancing cats,

prancing cats.

Bubble cats,

double cats.

Flying cats,

trying cats.

Cats that wink,

cats that think.

Cats,

cats,

cats.

I love cats!

Snuggly cats,

bubbly cats.

Juggling cats,

tumbling cats.

Singing cats,

swinging cats.

Cats in your pocket,

cats in the drawer.

Cats in the kitchen,

cats
at the
door.

Cats are friends,

cats are mates.

Cuddly cats or crazy cats . . .

Cats
are
great!

Cats,
cats,
cats.

I love cats!